Merry Christmas, Sugar!

By Ellie O'Ryan
Illustrated by Sachiho Hino

ANGEL CAT SUGAR
characters created by Yuko Shimizu

SCHOLASTIC INC.

New York Toronto London Auckland Sydney Mexico City New Delhi Hong Kong

ISBN 978-0-545-23435-1

ANGEL CAT SUGAR © 2010 YUKO SHIMIZU/TACT.C.INC.

ANGEL CAT SUGAR and all related characters and elements are
trademarks of and © YUKO SHIMIZU/TACT.C.INC. All rights reserved.

Published by Scholastic Inc. SCHOLASTIC and associated logos
are trademarks and/or registered trademarks of Scholastic Inc.

12 11 10 9 8 7 6 5 4 3 2 1   10 11 12 13 14/0

Printed in the U.S.A. 40
First printing, September 2010

It was almost Christmas, and Angel Cat Sugar was so excited!
She had searched all over Misty Mountain for the perfect pine tree.
She couldn't wait to decorate it!

But first Sugar had to help her littlest friend, Cinnamon, decorate *his* house!

Cinnamon lived in a shoe box in Sugar's bedroom. Sugar made lots of teeny-tiny decorations. She hung strands of beads on the walls. Then she put an itty-bitty star on top of a twig from her Christmas tree. At last Cinnamon's house was ready for Christmas!

Helping Cinnamon decorate his house was so much fun that it gave Sugar a great idea. "Maybe my friends would like to help decorate my Christmas tree!" she said.

So Sugar bundled up and set off down the snowy path to Thyme's house.

Thyme was so happy to see Sugar! "Hi, Sugar!" he called. "You're just in time to help me decorate this gingerbread house!"

Sugar clapped her hands excitedly. "It's beautiful!" she exclaimed. Th covered the house with yummy candies. It looked good enough to eat!

When they were done, Sugar said, "Thyme, would you like to help decorate my Christmas tree?"

Thyme shook his head. "I wish I could!" he replied. "But I still have to finish decorating all these cookies!"

Sugar walked down the snowy path again. Soon she reached her friend Parsley's house. *Maybe he would like to help decorate my tree,* thought Sugar.

"Hi, Sugar!" Parsley said. "It looks cold out there. Come in!"

Sugar stepped into Parsley's cheerful living room. "I'm making Christmas cards," Parsley explained. "Want to help?"

"Sure!" Sugar exclaimed. She helped Parsley make a colorful stack of
cards for his friends. Then she said, "Parsley, would you like to help decorate
my Christmas tree?"

"I would—but I have to deliver all these cards," Parsley replied.

Snowflakes fluttered down from the sky as Sugar and Parsley walked to their friend Basil's house. Parsley slipped a card in Basil's mailbox and continued on the path, while Sugar rang the doorbell.

"Hello, Sugar!" Basil said. "I'm making Christmas wreaths."
"Wow!" Sugar said. "I've never made a wreath before."
"Come inside and I can show you how to do it!" Basil replied.

Basil showed Sugar how to weave the green branches into pretty wreaths. Then they added red winterberries from Basil's garden to each one!

"All these branches remind me why I came over today," Sugar said. "Would you like to help decorate my Christmas tree?" she asked.

"That sounds like fun!" replied Basil. "But I still have to make bows for the wreaths. Sorry, Sugar!"

Night started to fall as Sugar walked home. Her house was dark and quiet.

It's nighttime already!
It's too late to decorate this
big tree all by *myself*, Sugar
thought sadly.

Suddenly, Sugar heard voices singing in the frosty night.
She opened the door to find Parsley, Basil, and Thyme caroling on her doorste

"Merry Christmas, Sugar!" everyone said.
"Can we still help decorate your Christmas tree?" asked Basil.
"Of course!" Sugar said. "Please come in!"
"I'll hang this wreath on your door," Basil said.
"Does anyone want a cookie?" asked Thyme.
"Here's your Christmas card, Sugar!" said Parsley.

Sugar smiled as her friends came inside.
Everyone gathered around the tree to loop strands of lights
around the branches. Then they carefully hung the ornaments.

When they were finished, the lights on the Christmas tree twinkle making all the ornaments sparkle a shine. Sugar's house was warm and cozy with all her friends. And that made it the merriest Christmas ever